T.R. Bear

T.R. GOES TO HOLLYWOOD

Terrance Dicks
Illustrated by Susan Hellard

Piccadilly Press · London

Phototypeset by V.I.P. Type Ltd., Milton Keynes, Bucks.
Printed and bound by Adlard & Son Ltd.,
for the publishers, Piccadilly Press Ltd.,
5 Canfield Place, London NW6 3BT

British Library Cataloguing in Publication Data

Dicks, Terrance
T.R. Goes to Hollywood—(T. R. Bear, v. 8)
I. Title   II. Hellard, Susan   III. Series
823'.914 [J]   PZ7
ISBN 1 85340 004 1

Other books in the series
T.R. BEAR – ENTER T.R.
T.R. BEAR – T.R. GOES TO SCHOOL
T.R. BEAR – T.R.'s DAY OUT
T.R. BEAR – T.R. AFLOAT
T.R. BEAR – T.R.'s HALLOWE'EN
T.R. BEAR – T.R.'s BIG GAME
T.R. BEAR – T.R.'s FESTIVAL

Terrance Dicks – British – is the producer of the BBC TV Classics series.
He is a well-known writer, and among the other series he has done for
Piccadilly Press are: *Sally Ann*, *Buster and Betsy*, and
The Adventures of David and Goliath.
He lives in the Hampstead, London.

Susan Hellard – British – is an increasingly popular illustrator.
All her illustrations possess a wry sense of humour.
She has illustrated the *Dilly* series and a number of picture
books for Piccadilly Press. She lives in the Crouch End, London.

Chapter One

Pie in the Sky

The air hostess leaned over Jimmy's seat and flashed him a big, toothy smile.

'Why, hi there little feller. You want me to bring a tray for your teddy bear too?'

'No thanks,' said Jimmy politely. 'T.R. will share mine.'

'Is that his name – T.R.?'

'He's named after one of your American presidents – Theodore Roosevelt.'

1

The air hostess studied the teddy bear in the empty seat next to Jimmy. 'Well, isn't he cute?' The bear scowled straight ahead.

It was short and tubby, and it wore a check hunting jacket, a bow tie, and round wire spectacles with no glass in them. It really didn't look cute at all though – more like tough and determined.

The stewardess put the plastic

tray of airline food down on the little table that unfolded from the seat in front, ruffled Jimmy's hair and went on her way.

As soon as she was gone T.R. growled, 'You shoudda taken her up on the offer, kid. I'm starving.'

'Don't worry, I'm not really hungry. You can have most of mine.'

To tell the truth, Jimmy was still too excited to be hungry.

He had a very good reason for being excited too.

Jimmy and T.R. were on a jet plane going to America.

Better still, they were going to Hollywood!

Not by themselves, of course.

Jimmy's mum and dad, not to mention his brother George and his sister Jenny, were coming along as well. They were all sitting in the row in front.

Their four seats were all in the centre section of the plane, while Jimmy and T.R. had three seats all to themselves a row behind on the left.

This arrangement suited Jimmy just fine, since it gave him and T.R. a bit of privacy and a chance for a chat. T.R., like most toys, had the power to come alive when he wanted to, but *un*like most toys, T.R. had a way of forgetting the rules and piping up when someone could hear him.

T.R. was in an even more excitable state than usual today. It was understandable enough, Jimmy thought.

For Jimmy himself, the American trip was a wonderful adventure. But as far as T.R. was concerned he was going home.

T.R. was an all-American bear, named after and modelling himself on Theodore Roosevelt, as Jimmy had just told the stewardess. He'd been sent as a present from Jimmy's uncle in America, and now he was on his way back.

T.R. sank luxuriously back into his seat. 'This sure beats my last trip, kid, wrapped up in a parcel and stuck in the baggage hold. This is living! What's on that meal tray?'

Jimmy studied the plastic tray. It was divided into different sections, each one containing a different item of cellophane-wrapped food. 'Some kind of meat – looks like beef. Vegetables, salad, orange juice, pie, roll and butter and a cup for coffee – I suppose they'll be bringing that round.'

'I'll take the OJ and the pie,' said T.R. 'The rest is all yours.'

Jimmy unwrapped the food and they started to eat.

They were all on their way to a children's books convention in Los Angeles.

Jimmy's father, who wrote children's history books, had been invited to attend and give a speech, and he'd decided to take the whole family and make it a holiday.

As they munched away Jimmy said, 'Listen, T.R., is Hollywood in Los Angeles, or Los Angeles in Hollywood, or what?'

'The city's called Los Angeles – L.A. for short. Hollywood's just part of it – ' T.R. shut up hurriedly as the hostess came back and poured coffee into Jimmy's plastic cup.

Suddenly they heard an angry voice coming from further down the plane. 'Listen, do you know who I am? I'm Larry Dome, President of

MegaDome Productions. How dare
you talk to me like that!'

Jimmy leaned out and looked
down the aisle and saw their
stewardess arguing with a short,
bald-headed, bespectacled man,
who was smoking a huge cigar.

'We're very honoured to have
you on board, Mr Dome,' said the
hostess soothingly. 'But I'm afraid
you still can't smoke your cigar,
even here in the smoking section.
No pipes and no cigars, that's the
rule.'

The man argued some more, but the hostess was firm, and eventually he gave in and put out the cigar.

As the hostess came back down the aisle Jimmy said, 'Well done, you certainly told him.'

The air hostess grinned. 'I wouldn't care, but MegaDome is one of the smallest studios in Hollywood. To hear him talk, you'd think it was MGM and Warners rolled into one!'

It takes a very long time to get to America, even in a jet plane, but for T.R. and Jimmy the time passed quickly enough.

After the meal there was the movie. The air hostess came round with headphones which you plugged into a socket in the arm of your seat. Then she pulled down a screen from the ceiling and the film started. It was the new James Bond film, and Jimmy and T.R. thoroughly enjoyed it.

After the film the main lights were dimmed and everyone had a little nap.

Everyone but T.R. He was still wide awake.

Suddenly he heard stealthy footsteps moving down the aisle. Someone moved past him, heading for the front of the plane.

T.R. leaned out and peered down the darkened aisle.

He saw a skinny little man sneak down the aisle and slip into an empty seat, next to the man who'd made such a fuss about his cigar.

The bald man still had his overhead reading light on, and it shone down on the two men like a little spotlight. They had their heads together in an urgent, whispered conference, and somehow T.R. just *knew* they were up to no good.

T.R. jumped down from his seat and scurried along the aisle towards them. He nipped under the skinny man's seat and listened hard.

'Trust me Mr Dome, it's all fixed,' the skinny man was saying. 'I've been slipping our guys into the studio for weeks now. I got a call from the man in charge just before we caught this plane. Everything's set.'

'It had better work,' growled Larry Dome.

'Trust me,' said the skinny man again. 'It can't miss. That first studio tour is going to be a total disaster.'

Larry Dome chuckled evilly. 'I like it, Sidney. The day Sweetheart Studios open their tour – they lose their whole studio. Another couple of days and the whole place will be mine!'

Chapter Two

Dangerous Tour

'Here it is,' said T.R. 'Right here in Variety'.

It was the next day, and they were sitting in the foyer of their hotel.

The hotel was an amazing place. The foyer was as high as the hotel itself with the rooms built round it in a circle.

Glass lifts ran up the inside of the circle and the foyer had a fountain and a little forest of palm trees.

T.R. and Jimmy were sitting in a quiet little alcove, waiting for the others to come down from their rooms. They'd all been too tired to do much the day before, but now they were all ready to set off on their first day out. Jimmy's father's conference didn't start until tomorrow.

T.R. was reading a sort of giant newspaper, with shiny pages like a magazine.

'Here what is?' asked Jimmy.

'This is Variety,' explained T.R. 'The show-biz newspaper. Listen!'

He began reading aloud.

' "Struggling Sweetheart Studios still fighting off MegaDome buyout bid. Today Sweetheart start studio tours in fund-raising foray. Meanwhile work continues on 'Dino,' new monster pic tipped to save Sweetheart's flagging fortunes." '

'I think I need a translation,' said Jimmy.

'C'mon, kid, you remember Sweetheart Studios. Sort of a mini Walt Disney outfit.'

'Didn't they make those Buster Bear cartoons? And all those

adventure films with kids and animals in?'

'That's right. The studio hasn't been doing too well lately, and this other outfit MegaDome have been trying to buy them out. But MegaDome make nasties, yukky horror movies, so Sweetheart don't wanna know. Besides, Sweetheart are making this big new movie about a kid with a pet dinosaur. If it's a smash, the studio will be back in the money.'

'This is all very interesting, T.R.' said Jimmy politely. 'But what's it got to do with us?'

'Listen,' said T.R. again, and for the first time he told Jimmy about the conversation he'd overheard on the plane. 'That guy Dome must be planning some kind of dirty work.

We've gotta do something about it.'

'We could warn the studios,' suggested Jimmy. 'Ring up or something. Or we could tell the police.'

'Do you think anyone would listen – to a boy and a bear? Nope, there's only one thing for it, kid. We gotta go on that tour and catch the bad guys in the act. C'mon, pick me up. We'll go over to the tourist desk.'

It was no use arguing with T.R. when he was in this mood. He was like the sheriff in a Western, riding into town to clean things up. Meekly Jimmy obeyed.

At the desk a nice, motherly, silver-haired lady sold Jimmy a ticket for the tour. 'The studio bus goes round all the big hotels. It'll be picking up here in about ten minutes.'

They went back towards the fountain and found the rest of the family had arrived. They were already wrangling about where to go first.

His parents wanted to go to a big art museum, his sister Jenny wanted to see the shops, and brother George wanted to do a tour of movie star homes.

'Where do you two want to go?' asked Jimmy's dad wearily. 'Nowhere anyone else does, I bet!'

'Don't worry about us,' said Jimmy hurriedly. 'T.R. and I are all fixed up!' And once his parents realised the tour was properly organised and that there'd be a guide with them all the time, they agreed to let them go.

'Welcome to Sweetheart Studios,'
said the tall, fair-haired young man,
'one of the oldest film studios in
Hollywood, and still one of the best.
My grandad founded it, sixty years
ago, and I'm President today. My name's
Jay Hart, and I'm going to be your
guide on this first-ever Sweetheart
Studio Tour . . . So if you'll all
climb on board the trolley . . .'

'That's the guy we gotta talk to,'

growled T.R. He was riding in
Jimmy's old school bag as usual,
and Jimmy was standing at the

front of the little group of tourists assembled outside Sweetheart Studios, which seemed to consist of a scattered group of rather run-down single-storey buildings, spread out over quite a large area.

The tour trolley was like a longish road train. The open cars had benches running down the centre, so the passengers sat facing outwards, back to back. It was pulled by a little electric truck rather like a giant dodgem car, which was disguised as a steam engine, complete with fake funnel.

The fair-haired young man jumped in the seat next to the driver.

He spoke into a microphone, so that his voice boomed down the length of the trolley. 'All aboard? Then away we go!'

Jimmy had made a dash for the front seat of the front car, so he was sitting just behind Jay Hart and the driver.

As the trolley set off, he tapped Jay on the shoulder. 'Excuse me, I've got to talk to you . . .'

'Not now, kid,' said Jay hurriedly. 'Try me later.'

His voice boomed from the speakers. 'These days, ladies and gentlemen, we go all over the world to make our movies. But when films first started out, movies set all over the world, any place and any time, were all filmed right here in Hollywood, on what we call the back lot. First stop, the old wild west!'

The driver swung round a corner and suddenly they were in the kind of Western street Jimmy had seen in a hundred films and TV shows.

Wooden buildings and a wooden boardwalk, a saloon, a jailhouse, the stables and the general store, they were all there.

Suddenly two men in cowboy clothes rushed out of the swing doors of the saloon. They squared

up to each other in the dusty main
street and then went for their guns.

The air was filled with the sound
of pistol-shots!

'Looks like trouble,' shouted Jay.
'We'd better get out of town!'

The trolley rattled down the
street, turned the corner – and they
found themselves facing a
wobbly-looking wooden bridge
over a rushing river. 'We've gotta
get over that bridge, folks,' shouted
Jay. 'It looks pretty rickety though.
Will we make it?'

The bridge swayed and creaked
alarmingly as they rushed towards
it.

Jimmy grinned. 'Don't worry, T.R., it's all part of the tour!'

'Watch that driver, kid,' yelled T.R. 'He's up to something!'

As Jimmy watched, the driver wrenched the wheel hard so that the trolley was heading not for the bridge but straight for the river.

Then he jumped from his seat, hit the ground and rolled over and ran off.

'Look out!' yelled Jimmy, but Jay had his back to the driver to talk to the tourists and had seen nothing.

'What do you think, folks?' he shouted cheerfully. 'Are we gonna make it?'

The driverless trolley headed straight towards the rushing torrent . . .

Chapter Three

Ride of Terror

Jimmy jumped over the low partition, his bag with T.R. still round his neck, scrambled into the driver's seat and grabbed the wheel. Jimmy wrenched it round so that the trolley was headed for the bridge again.

Jay swung round. 'What the heck's going on? Where's the driver?'

'He's abandoned ship,' gasped

Jimmy. 'Tell you later!'

Jay reached for the wheel, then changed his mind. 'Too late to change places, kid. You'll have to take her over. Just keep us in the middle of the bridge . . .'

They were actually on the bridge by now, and it was creaking and swaying alarmingly, lurching from side to side as if caught in a hurricane.

As they shot past, one of the big side timbers broke away and crashed into the river below.

'Don't worry,' yelled Jay. 'This is all supposed to happen – just special effects, like in the movies. The bridge is as safe as houses.'

The bridge might be safe, thought Jimmy, but that didn't mean to say that they were!

Holding the trolley to the middle of the bucking, swaying bridge was a job for a skilled driver – and Jimmy certainly wasn't that. If he lost control, they'd smash through the flimsy side-barrier and plummet to the river below.

Somehow or other, with T.R. shouting instructions over the noise of the river, Jimmy got the trolley across.

Once they were on safe ground he and Jay managed to change places, and Jay drove the trolley up to a big refreshment kiosk and parked outside.

Standing up, he turned and spoke to the excited passengers.

'Well, there you are folks, the bridge was so scary our driver jumped but the kid and the bear pulled us through. How about a round of applause?'

All the passengers cheered and whistled. Jimmy blushed and looked down at T.R. who was still in the school bag slung round his neck.

He was afraid T.R. would stand up and take a bow, but the little bear was still managing to lie doggo, though his glasses were

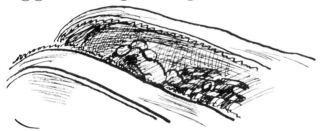

wonky. But he looked distinctly flustered, and he'd fallen back inside the bag.

'We'll take a short break now,' Jay went on. 'Coke, hot dogs, popcorn and souvenirs are all available at the stall!'

The passengers climbed off, all chattering excitedly, clearly convinced that everything that had happened was part of the tour.

Jay turned to Jimmy and said fiercely, 'Now, what the blue blazes is going on?'

'I tried to warn you earlier, but you wouldn't listen.'

'Well, I'm listening now!'

Jimmy heard a mutter from the school bag. 'So tell him, kid!'

Jimmy told him about the two men plotting on the plane. 'This friend of mine just happened to overhear them.'

'Will he give evidence against them? Testify in court?'

Jimmy couldn't help smiling at

the thought of T.R. in the witness
box. 'I don't think anyone would
believe him. He's er – even smaller
than I am. The main thing is,
you've got to cancel this tour before
something else happens.'

'No way, kid,' said Jay fiercely.
'That'd mean they'd won. This
tour's going ahead, on schedule. I'll
drive and do the commentary at the
same time. You can sit beside me
and keep your eyes peeled!'

He raised his voice. 'Time to be
on our way, folks, for the next stage
of this terrifying tour!'

Terrifying was the word, thought

Jimmy, as the tour set off. He heard a growl from inside the bag. 'Attaboy! We'll show'em! Wagons roll!'

Maybe this was the spirit that won the West, thought Jimmy. It was obvious that T.R.'s fighting spirit was roused. Jimmy himself felt like a scout on a wagon train through hostile Indian territory.

And who knew where the enemy would strike next . . .

For a while things went peacefully enough.

Jay drove them through an Old Chinatown street and then on to a Chicago street, filled with men in dark suits and black hats. Some of them were carrying violin cases. 'I don't think those guys are really musicians, folks,' boomed Jay

cheerily. 'Something tells me we're about to get caught in the middle of the Chicago gang wars. Let's hope the Untouchables aren't too far away!'

Sure enough, some of the men took machineguns from their violin cases and started blazing away at each other, with the trolley in the middle.

Jay turned to Jimmy. 'Don't

worry, they're only blanks!'

Suddenly a line of holes appeared in the striped awning above their heads. Jimmy nudged Jay and pointed. 'Looks as if one of your gangsters is using live ammunition!'

With a yell, Jay put his foot down, and the trolley shot out of the street and around the corner.

Suddenly they found themselves in the courtyard of a medieval castle.

Soldiers in old-fashioned uniforms were attacking a big wooden door with a battering ram. Up on the castle walls, other soldiers were yelling defiance.

'Good old Middle Ages stuff,' yelled Jay to Jimmy. 'Should be safe enough . . .'

Suddenly an arrow thudded into the wooden seat-back between them.

At the same moment, Jimmy, glancing upwards, saw two sinister figures tilting a huge steaming cauldron on the castle battlements just over their heads.

Grabbing the wheel from Jay's hand Jimmy wrenched it hard, swinging the trolley away from the

battlements – just as the boiling oil
from the cauldron splashed down
on the spot where they'd been . . .

Jay drove the trolley out of the
courtyard, through an arched
gateway, and suddenly they were
on a modern road again, with yet
another kiosk in front of them.

'Time for another refreshment
break, folks,' called Jay. 'We'll go on
in five minutes for the last and most
exciting part of the ride!'

Jimmy mopped his forehead. 'I hope it won't be any more exciting than this! What are those people trying to do?'

'Give one of our passengers a really bad fright,' said Jay. 'Even injure some of them, they wouldn't care. They want to make it look as if it was all our fault, as if we'd deliberately made the tour too dangerous. The injured passengers would sue for damages, we'd have to sell up and go out of business, and MegaDome could buy us up cheap.' He patted Jimmy on the back. 'Don't worry, we've beaten them, thanks to you. Only one more section to go.'

'What's that?' asked Jimmy nervously.

'It's the dinosaur we're using in

our new movie. A huge animated model.'

'So what happens?'

'The tour trolley drives through his cave, the dinosaur pops up and snarls and roars a bit, and we drive on. Nothing to it!'

As Jay herded the passengers back on board the trolley, T.R. said, 'Sit me up in the bag, kid, I don't want to miss the dinosaur!'

'I just hope the dinosaur misses us,' said Jimmy.

Jay jumped in the driving seat, and the tour trolley lurched on its way.

Jay drove them straight towards a low cliff, with a rocky tunnel opening in the centre.

'This is the way into the dinosaur's cave, folks. They say he's a friendly dinosaur though. Let's hope they're right!'

Jimmy looked down at T.R. 'Hear, hear!' he whispered.

T.R. was standing upright in the bag, gazing excitedly ahead. 'Some fun, eh kid?' The trolley rattled into the gloomy tunnel.

Chapter Four

T.R. Meets a Monster

Although it was fairly gloomy in the tunnel, it wasn't completely dark. The rocky walls seemed to glow with an eerie green light.

Studying them closely, Jimmy saw the walls weren't rock at all, they were plastic with some kind of light behind them.

The tunnel led right into a darker cave area.

'This is it, folks,' boomed Jay.

'The dinosaur's lair! Will he let us by alive?'

Suddenly the cave lit up revealing an enormous dinosaur, rearing up ahead of them.

The model was life size, so well made that it seemed absolutely real. 'Say, that's terrific!' said T.R.

Assuming Jimmy was speaking, Jay said proudly, 'Latest thing in electronic animation. It's all computerised, controlled from inside.'

The dinosaur swung its massive head in anger, opening its enormous mouth to reveal a throat like a tunnel and rows of jagged teeth.

It gave a shattering roar, and twitched its long tail to and fro.

Waving its clawed front legs, it

stumped towards them on its massive back paws.

There came a sudden rumble behind them.

'It's a rock fall, folks,' yelled Jay. 'We can't go back, now we have to go on!' He winked at Jimmy and whispered, 'All part of the tour, like the fake bridge.'

'What happens now?' whispered Jimmy.

'The dinosaur stumps a bit nearer. Then he moves to one side, and roars as we drive past. He'll be stopping just about – now!'

But the dinosaur didn't stop. It lurched straight towards the trolley, now halted in the tunnel, unable to go forward or back.

'It isn't going to stop!' yelled Jay. 'Someone's interfered with its

programming. That thing weighs *tons*. It'll crush the trolley and everyone in it!'

The dinosaur lurched closer . . .

Suddenly Jimmy became aware that T.R. was punching him on the arm.

'Get me outta this bag, kid!'

Jimmy lifted him out. 'Don't be scared, T.R.'

'Who's scared?' demanded T.R. indignantly. 'Now, jump down and run up to the dinosaur. Get a move on!'

Clutching T.R. in his arms, Jimmy ran up to the dinosaur, now

very close to the trolley.

'Now throw me into its jaws,' yelled T.R.

Jimmy stared at him. 'What?'

'Just do it, kid. Trust me!'

Jimmy drew back his arm and hurled T.R. straight into the dinosaur's gaping jaws.

By now he'd worked out what T.R. was up to, and he was determined to help.

Running back to the trolley, ignoring the astonished Jay and the excitedly squealing passengers, Jimmy climbed up onto the top of the ornamental canopy over the driver's seat.

The dinosaur was very close now.

It lurched forwards, its gaping jaws only a few feet above him.

With a flying leap, Jimmy followed T.R. into the jaws of the dinosaur.

Its throat was as big as a giant drainpipe and scraping over the plastic teeth, Jimmy disappeared inside. It was rather like going down the water-chute at the baths.

But this chute ended not in a pool, but in a tiny control room,

rather like the cockpit of a plane.

The skinny man who T.R. had seen talking to Larry Dome on the plane was crouching over a control console. Above his head, a monitor screen showed the view through the dinosaur's eyes – a trolley-load of terrified tourists, with Jay standing bravely in front of them to protect them.

T.R. was standing on top of the console yelling, 'Quit that, buster! Get away from those controls!'

The astonished Skinny aimed a blow at him, but T.R. dodged back.

'Leave him to me, T.R.,' shouted Jimmy.

He jumped up on top of the console, then off again, straight at Skinny, catching him under the chin with two bony knees.

Skinny fell backwards with a yell, Jimmy on top of him, and went limp as they hit the ground.

Realising Skinny must have knocked himself out, Jimmy scrambled free.

T.R. was running up and down the console, stabbing at controls. 'Okay, kid, I've got the hang of it now.'

The view on the monitor screen changed as the dinosaur lurched backwards, allowing the trolley to get past.

Jimmy and T.R. found an exit – there was a trapdoor in the dinosaur's tummy – and were just in time to jump up next to Jay as the trolley drove away . . .

*   *   *

'Well, you sure saved the day for

us,' said Jay, as the happy tourists
went off, chattering excitedly about
their ride. He looked at T.R. 'Say,
did I see that bear talk – and move?'

'Oh, just a bit of electronic
animation,' said Jimmy hurriedly.
'It's a hobby of mine.'

'Listen,' said Jay, 'I've got a lot to
do, rounding up the bad guys and
making sure the next tour runs
smoothly. I don't want to go
through *that* ride again. I just can't
thank you enough, kid. If there's

anything I can do for you . . .'

'Think nothing of it,' said Jimmy hurriedly. 'We enjoyed it, didn't we T.R.?'

'Sure thing,' said T.R. 'Most fun I've had in years!'

Jay gave him an astonished look, and Jimmy said hurriedly, 'If you could just show us where to get the bus back to the hotel . . .'

'Bus?' said Jay indignantly. 'After what you've done for this studio? Kid, you and your bear are travelling in style . . .'

*   *   *

Jimmy's mum and dad and brother and sister were standing outside the hotel, waiting for Jimmy and T.R.

Suddenly, the most enormous limousine they'd ever seen swept up the drive. It was low and black and

gleaming with smoked windows,
an it looked about as long as a bus.

'Look at that,' said Jimmy's
brother George enviously.

'I bet it's a famous film star,' said
his sister Jenny.

'Or some big-shot Hollywood
producer,' said his dad.

'Oh no it isn't', said his mother
wonderingly. 'Look!'

The limousine drew up in front
of them.

A very tall black-uniformed
chauffeur got out, walked round to
the passenger door and opened it

with a flourish, bowing low.

Out stepped Jimmy, school bag round his neck, with T.R. staring proudly ahead.

Jimmy looked at his astonished family.

'Is it time for lunch yet?' he said hopefully. 'T.R. and I are starving!'